Topic: Transportation and Safety   **Subtopic:** Traffic Crossings

Notes to Parents and Teachers:

As a child becomes more familiar reading books, it is important for him/her to rely on and use reading strategies more independently to help figure out words they don't know.

REMEMBER: PRAISE IS A GREAT MOTIVATOR!

Here are some praise points for beginning readers:

- I saw you get your mouth ready to say the first letter of that word.
- I like the way you used the picture to help you figure out that word.
- I noticed that you saw some sight words you knew how to read!

Book Ends for the Reader!

Here are some reminders before reading the text:

- Point to each word you read to make it match what you say.
- Use the picture for help.
- Look at and say the first letter sound of the word.
- Look for sight words that you know how to read in the story.
- Think about the story to see what word might make sense.

Words to Know Before You Read

cars

color

drive

go

green

light

red

street

RED LIGHT, GREEN LIGHT

By
Michael Taylor

Illustrated by Srimalie Bassani

Rourke
Educational Media

rourkeeducationalmedia.com

Look at the light. What color is it?

Is it red or green?

5

It is red! Dad stops the car.

6

A boy crosses the street.

Look at the light. What color is it?

Is it red or green?

It is green! We can go.

Drive away slowly.

Look at the light.
What color is it?

Is it red or green?

It is red! Stop! Don't cross the street.

See the fast cars go by?

15

Look at the light. What color is it?

Is it red or green?

It is green! I can go.

18

Wait! Check both ways first.

Look left. Look right.

A girl is in the car.

Book Ends for the Reader

I know...

1. What color lights are there on a traffic light?

2. What do cars do when their traffic light is red?

3. What do cars do when their traffic light is green?

I think ...

1. When you cross the road, do you look at the traffic lights carefully?

2. When can you cross the road?

3. Can you run as soon as the light changes?

What happened in this book?

Look at each picture and talk about what happened in the story.

About the Author

Michael Taylor is a retired teacher of 35 years. Throughout his teaching career he always had a passion for writing. The author of over 30 children's books, he now spends his free time hiking, fishing, and traveling but still enjoys creating fun, whimsical books for kids.

About the Illustrator

Since Srimalie was a child her mother gave her the passion for drawing and painting, and she had always encouraged her artistic expression. Her work is always full of surprises. It's difficult to remove her from her writing desk, where she keeps a stack of books, pages, tea cups of many colors and also amuses her fat cat.

Library of Congress PCN Data

Red Light, Green Light / Michael Taylor

ISBN 978-1-68342-715-5 (hard cover)(alk.paper)
ISBN 978-1-68342-767-4 (soft cover)
ISBN 978-1-68342-819-0 (e-Book)
Library of Congress Control Number: 2017935360

Rourke Educational Media
Printed in the United States of America, North Mankato, Minnesota

Edited by: Debra Ankiel
Art direction and layout by: Rhea Magaro-Wallace
Cover and interior Illustrations by: Srimalie Bassani